What Forest Knows

A Richard Jackson Book

A Atheneum Books for Young Readers
atheneum New York London Toronto Sydney New Delhi

by George
Ella Lyon

illustrated by
August Hall

ATHENEUM BOOKS FOR YOUNG READERS

An imprint of Simon & Schuster Children's Publishing Division

1230 Avenue of the Americas, New York, New York 10020

For information about special discounts for bulk purchases,
please contact Simon & Schuster Special Sales at 1-866-506-1949
or business@simonandschuster.com.

The Simon & Schuster Speakers Bureau can bring authors to your
live event. For more information or to book an event, contact the
Simon & Schuster Speakers Bureau at 1-866-248-3049 or visit our
website at www.simonspeakers.com.

Book design by Debra Sfetsios-Conover

The text for this book is set in Chaloops Galaxy.

The illustrations for this book are rendered in Photoshop, and
some of them are created over photographs.

Manufactured in China

0914 SCP

First Edition

10 9 8 7 6 5 4 3 2 1

Library of Congress Cataloging-in-Publication Data

Lyon, George Ella, 1949–

What Forest knows / George Ella Lyon ; illustrated by August Hall.
— First edition.

p. cm

"A Richard Jackson Book."

Summary: Follows the changing seasons in a forest as trees and
animals are nourished and are dependent on each other.

ISBN 978-1-4424-6775-0 (hardcover)

ISBN 978-1-4424-6776-7 (eBook)

[1. Trees—Fiction. 2. Forest ecology—Fiction. 3. Ecology—
Fiction. 4. Nature—Fiction. 5. Seasons—Fiction.] I. Hall, August,
illustrator. II. Title.

PZ7.L9954Wg 2014

[E]—dc23

2013045227

For

Wyatt Bradford Cook,

Ernst Jeffrey Ramsey, Solomon David Schwartzman,

Samuel Abraham Schwartzman, Nina Kendrick Strickland, and

Virginia Breedlove Yankie:

Root deep, reach high,
and know that you belong.

*

"The last word in ignorance is the man who says of an animal or plant, 'What good is it?'
If the land mechanism as a whole is good, then every part is good, whether we understand it or not."
—Aldo Leopold, *Round River*
—G. E. L.

I'd like to thank Debra Sfetsios-Conover and Allen Spiegel for the opportunity to illustrate this book.
And a big thank-you to the forest.
—A. H.

FOREST knows snow—

icy branches
frozen waterfall

squirrels asleep in hollows

insects burrowed in bark

moles resting among roots

Forest knows waiting,

holding on.

Forest knows buds—

soft life pushing through

hard wood,

a haze
of yellow-green, purple, pink
above cascading creeks.

Warblers, woodpeckers, bluebirds
sing spring songs,
weave nests.

Foxes, wolves, deer
nest too.

Forest knows waking,
opening up.

Forest knows leaves,
held out like hands,

cupping sunlight,
turning it to food,
reaching, stretching

while creeks
wriggle on to rivers.

Birds fledge,
possums wobble from the nest.

Bees buzz off
to find flowers.

Centipedes ripple
from dirt at the roots
to try all those new legs.

Forest knows growing,
going forth.

Forest knows fruit—

berries, nuts, cones
to seed new trees

and feed forest folk
through winter.

When red and gold leaves
swirl to the ground,
squirrels hide nuts,
birds fly south,
foxes and rabbits fatten.

Insects burrow in.
Bears den up
for the long sleep.

Forest knows
gathering in,
letting go.

Then Forest knows snow.

While Earth
travels
round the sun

Forest knows
each season,
each creature
needs the others.

Make friends
with a path
threading
through woods.

Listen.
Look.

Sniff.

Forest knows
everything belongs.

YOU, too.